ZONDERVAN.com/
AUTHORTRACKER
follow your favorite authors

ZONDERkidz

Living
Lights

ZONDERKIDZ

The Berenstain Bears® Follow God's Word
Copyright © 2011 by Berenstain Bears, Inc.
Illustrations © 2011 by Berenstain Bears, Inc.

Requests for information should be addressed to:
Zonderkidz, *Grand Rapids, Michigan 49530*

ISBN 978-0-310-72591-6

The Berenstain Bears® God Loves You! ISBN 9780310712503 (2008)
The Berenstain Bears® and the Golden Rule ISBN 9780310712473 (2008)
The Berenstain Bears® Kindness Counts ISBN 9780310712472 (2010)
The Berenstain Bears® Go To Sunday School ISBN 9780310712480 (2008)
The Berenstain Bears® and the Gift of Courage ISBN 9780310712466 (2008)

Editor: Mary Hassinger
Cover and interior design: Cindy Davis

Printed in China

11 12 13 14 15 16 /LPC/ 11 10 9 8 7 6 5 4 3

The Berenstain Bears® FOLLOW GOD'S WORD

written by Jan and Mike Berenstain

The Berenstain Bears®

God Loves You!

written by Jan and Mike Berenstain

ZONDERVAN.com/
AUTHORTRACKER
follow your favorite authors

ZONDERkidz

Living
Lights™

"God is love"
—1 John 4:16

The first week of school was a busy time for Brother and Sister Bear. It was a time to see old friends, meet new teachers, get their first homework assignments, and sign up for after-school activities.

Sister decided to try out for the big school show. This year it was *The Music Bear*. Sister thought she would be perfect in a leading role. She liked to sing "I Feel Pretty" from *Bearside Story* at home. Mama and Papa always said she was very good.

But there would be a lot of other girls trying out for the show too. Babs Bruno had a very fine voice, and there was Queenie McBear, of course. She thought she was the best singer in the school, and all her friends agreed with her.

THE
MUSIC BEAR
Tryouts

Sister

Brother Bear was trying out too, but not for the school show. He wanted to be on the school basketball team. He was pretty sure he could make it. He had been practicing dribbling and layups in the driveway at home. He played 21 with Papa after supper and always beat him.

Basketball Tryouts

Brother Be

The tryouts for the school play and basketball team were on the same day. After school, Brother went down to the gym and got into a basketball uniform. He and the other boys charged out onto the court and started warming up.

Sister joined a long line of cubs in the auditorium. Teacher Jane called them up on the stage one by one to sing a song. Babs sang "Memory," and she was very good. But Queenie made a mess of "Tomorrow"! She had a hard time hitting all the high notes. In spite of that, all her friends clapped and cheered, and Queenie took a few bows. Sister glanced over at Teacher Jane. She didn't look too impressed.

When it was Sister's turn, she sang "I Feel Pretty" just like she did at home for Mama and Papa.

In the gym, Brother was puffing and panting away, trying hard to look good. One after another, the boys dribbled, passed, shot layups, and took foul shots while Coach Grizzmeyer looked on and checked off names on a clipboard. You couldn't tell anything by watching him. His face never changed—never a smile, never a frown, not even a wink. The cubs called him Old Stoneface.

Finally, he said, "Okay, men! That's enough! The roster will be posted on the bulletin board outside my office tomorow."

On his way back to the locker room, Brother couldn't resist stopping to ask, "Coach, do you think I have a shot making the team?"

Coach Grizzmeyer just shrugged and said "We'll see, son."

In the auditorium, the auditions for the school show were winding up. Teacher Jane smiled a lot more than Coach Grizzmeyer, but she wasn't giving anything away, either.

"That's all for today, everyone!" she said. "I'll post my choices for the entire cast tomorrow on the bulletin board outside my room."

As Sister left, she couldn't resist stopping to ask, "Teacher Jane, do you think I have a chance of getting one of the main parts?"

But Teacher Jane just smiled and said, "We'll see, my dear."

Sister joined up with Brother as he walked home from school.

"Well, how do you think it went?" asked Sister. "Do you think you made the team?"

"Yeah, I think so!" said Brother hopefully. He really felt he had done well. He knew he was still a little short to be playing on the school team. But he hoped his skills and his hustle would make up for that.

"What about you?" Brother asked. "How did the auditions go?"

"Great, I think," said Sister.

"What did Teacher Jane think?" Brother asked.

"I don't know," said Sister thoughtfully. "She didn't say anything. She just smiled at everybody."

"At least she smiled. Old Stoneface never smiles!"

Sister laughed as they reached their tree house and climbed the steps.

"Oh, well!" she said, shrugging. "We'll find out how we did tomorrow."

And they did …

The next morning, both Brother and Sister rushed downstairs, gobbled their breakfasts, waved a quick good-bye to Mama and Papa, and got to school faster than they ever had before. They couldn't wait to see how they had done.

Brother rushed to Coach Grizzmeyer's office while Sister scurried to Teacher Jane's room. There were crowds of cubs gathered around the bulletin boards. Brother and Sister struggled to get up close.

Basketball TEAM LINEUP

Barry Bruin
Cousin Fred
Too-Tall Grizzly
Bob Bruno
Vinnie Bearkin
Chuck Ursullini
Sam Honeytree
Ralph O'Grizz
Lou Bearens

Chuck
Sam Honey
Ralph O'Griz
Lou Bearens
Brother Bear: Team Manager

Brother glanced quickly down the list of names. There was his, right at the bottom. At first, he felt a rush of relief. But then, he noticed what it said next to his name: Team Manager.

Team manager! TEAM MANAGER? The team manager just picked up basketballs and made sure everybody got on the bus on time. That's not what he wanted to do! He wanted to play; he wanted to shoot and dribble and dunk. He wanted to be a big star!

Crushed, he slunk down the hallway to his classroom.

THE MUSIC BEAR CAST

Ferdy Factual: Henry Hill
Babs Bruno: Marian
Ziggy Grizowsky: The Mayor
Queenie McBear: Mrs. Paroo
Harry Bearkis: Eddie
Bonnie Brown: Eulalie
Anna Grizzle: Gracie
Ron Ursowitz: Mr. Wash...
Sister Bear:

...e: Gracie
...owitz: Mr Washburn

Sister Bear:
Stage Manager

Outside Teacher Jane's room, Sister quickly looked over the cast. At first, she didn't see her name at all. Then she spotted it, right at the bottom.

Sister Bear: Stage Manager.

Stage manager! STAGE MANAGER? All the stage manager did was put away the props and make sure everybody got onstage on time. She didn't want to be stage manager. She wanted to act; she wanted to sing and dance and take bows. She wanted to be a big star!

Miserably, Sister trudged down the hall to her classroom.

When school let out that afternoon, Brother and Sister were both feeling very sorry for themselves. Even the weather seemed to be against them. Slowly, they climbed the front steps of the tree house.

Wearily, they plopped themselves down on the sofa in the living room. It seemed like the dark rain clouds outside had followed them in and were hanging over them.

"Whatever is the matter?" asked Mama.

"Yes," said Papa. "You both look like you are about to get a tooth drilled."

Brother and Sister sighed.

"Oh, we had a rough day at school," said Brother. "I didn't make the school basketball team."

"And I didn't get a part in the school show," added Sister, putting her chin in her hands.

"Oh, dear!" said Papa, concerned. "What a shame!"

"How disappointing!" said Mama. "Didn't Coach Grizzmeyer or Teacher Jane give you anything to do at all?"

"Well," said Brother, "they did give us something to do. I'm the team manager."

"And I'm the stage manager," said Sister. "But I don't want to do that! I want to be in the show!"

"And I want to be on the team!" said Brother.

"Well," said Mama, "I guess not everybody can be a star."

"But don't you think I deserve to be in the show?" asked Sister.

"Of course you do!" said Mama, giving her a hug. "You're a wonderful singer!"

"And don't you think I deserve to be on the team?" asked Brother.

"Of course you do!" said Papa, patting him on the shoulder. "You're a terrific basketball player!"

"I guess nobody else thinks so," said Sister gloomily. "I guess nobody at Bear Country School thinks much of us at all!" She heaved an even bigger sigh.

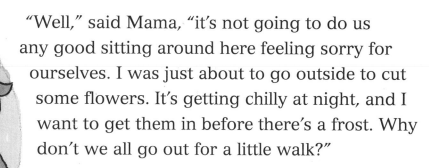

"Well," said Mama, "it's not going to do us any good sitting around here feeling sorry for ourselves. I was just about to go outside to cut some flowers. It's getting chilly at night, and I want to get them in before there's a frost. Why don't we all go out for a little walk?"

"But it's raining," protested Brother.

"The rain's stopped," said Papa, looking out the window. Sure enough, the clouds had lifted and the sun was peeking out.

Papa got Honey Bear into her stroller, and they all went outside. Mama stopped to cut some flowers at the back gate. They were very beautiful—big bright yellow, orange, pink, and violet blossoms. Birds were coming out after the rain and were singing in the trees. A big blue butterfly came sailing by and stopped to sip nectar from Mama's flowers. By now, the clouds had all rolled away and the golden sun was shining over the countryside.

"Look!" said Papa. "A rainbow!"

As the rays of the sun shone through the last drops of rain, a beautiful rainbow stretched right across the sky. "Wow!" said Brother. "It's so bright!"

"What makes a rainbow?" asked Sister in wonder.

"Well," said Papa, "you see ... the light from the sun shines through the raindrops and creates a prismatic thingy, which bounces around from the um ... uh ..."

Mama interrupted. "The rainbow is a gift from God. It's a sign that the rain is past and the sun has come to warm the earth again. God puts the rainbow in the sky as a beautiful sign of his love for all the earth and all the creatures that he has made."

"Even us?" asked Brother.

"Of course!" said Papa. "God loves everybody!"

"What about wasps?" asked Sister. A wasp had stung her in the school yard a few days ago, and she was very afraid of them.

"Well … yes," said Papa, shooing one away that was buzzing around Mama's flowers. "God loves all his creation!"

"Does he love us even when we're bad?" wondered Brother, a little puzzled.

"Well …" said Papa.

"What about when we're really, really bad?" asked Sister. "Like when Brother and I got into a fight and wouldn't speak to each other for a week?"

"Um …" said Papa.

"Or that time Too-Tall Grizzly and his gang dared me to steal Farmer Ben's watermelon?" asked Brother.

"Uh …" said Papa.

"Or when we watch too much TV?" put in Sister. "Or when I bite my nails? Or when we don't do our homework? Or when—"

"YES!" Mama broke in, suddenly. "He does!"

They all looked at her in surprise.

"You see," she explained patiently, "God wants us to be good. But he doesn't love us because we're good or bad. God loves us because he made us. It's a little bit like how mothers and fathers love their children."

"Oh," said Sister. "Like how you still love us even when we do things we're not supposed to?"

"That's right," said Papa. "Of course, we're disappointed when you misbehave. But we still love you! We even love you when you don't make the basketball team or get a part in the school show! And we're proud of you because your coach and teacher trusted you to be managers—special jobs for the most responsible cubs."

Brother and Sister smiled. They were beginning to feel slightly better about that little problem.

By now they had made their way down the lane to a spot that overlooked Farmer Ben's farm. It was a lovely scene. The cows were coming in from the pasture, the ducks were swimming in the pond, bees were buzzing around their hives, and the sun was setting behind the trees.

As the sky grew darker, they noticed a tiny point of light in the western sky.

"What's that?" wondered Brother.

"That's the evening star," said Papa. "It comes out just after sunset."

"Is that another sign of God's love?" asked Sister.

"Yes, dear," said Mama, giving her a hug. "It surely is!"

And, hand in hand, the Bear family turned for home and their evening meal.

The Berenstain Bears and the Golden Rule

written by Jan and Mike Berenstain

ZONDERVAN.com/
AUTHORTRACKER
follow your favorite authors

ZONDERkidz

Living Lights™

"Do to others what you would have them do to you"
—Matthew 7:12

Bear Country School

When Sister Bear received a beautiful golden locket for her birthday, she was surprised and pleased. It was shaped like a heart, and it had her name on it.

"Happy birthday, dear!" said Mama and Papa Bear, giving her a big hug.

Sister tried the locket on and looked at herself in the mirror. "I love it!" she said. "I'm going to wear it all the time."

"It opens up," said Papa. "Look!" He showed her the little golden clasp that you pressed to pop the locket open.

"Neat!" said Sister.

She looked inside,
expecting to find a little picture
or a mirror or something. But
all that she could see inside
the locket were a few simple
words: "Do to others what you
would have them do to you."

Sister was puzzled. The words
seemed familiar. But she wasn't sure
why. "What's this?" she asked.

"It's the golden rule," explained
Mama.

"What's that?" Sister wondered.

Mama's eyes widened. "The golden rule is one of the most important rules there is," she explained. "That's why we have always had it hanging up on the wall of our living room." She pointed to the framed sampler above their mantelpiece.

Sister gazed up at it in amazement. She had seen that sampler every day of her life. No wonder the words seemed familiar! "Oh," she said, a little embarrassed. "I never really thought about what it said before. What does it mean?"

"The golden rule," Papa explained, "tells you to treat other people the way you want to be treated yourself."

"Why is it inside my locket?" she wondered.

"It's a *golden* rule inside a *golden* locket for a little *golden* princess!" said Papa, giving her a big kiss.

"It's called the golden rule," explained Mama, patiently, "because it's precious, just like gold. But it's not about the gold you wear around your neck or on your finger." She held out her wedding ring. "It's about the golden treasure we keep inside our own hearts. The heart shape of the locket is meant to remind you of that."

Sister thought it over. She didn't really get it. But that was okay. She loved the new locket anyway.

The next day before school, Sister showed off her new treasure to her friends Lizzy, Millie, Anna, and Linda.

They oohed and ahhed over it in a very satisfying way. "What's all the fuss about?" asked a voice.

It was Queenie McBear and her gang. Queenie was older than Sister and a little snooty. When Queenie first came to the neighborhood, she and Sister did not get along at all. Queenie made fun of her and got Sister's friends to join in. That was Sister's first experience with an in-crowd—a group that makes itself feel big by making others feel small.

"Oh, hi Queenie," said Sister. "I was just showing the kids my new locket."

Over the years, Sister learned to get along with Queenie. But they never were the best of friends.

"Let's see!" said Queenie.

She looked the locket over. She was not impressed. She herself wore big hoop earrings and lots of beads and chains.

"Cute," was all she said as she walked away with her friends.

Queenie still had her own in-crowd. They were a group of the older girls who liked hanging out together and acting cool. Mostly, they spent their time painting their nails and giggling about boys.

That was okay with Sister. She had her own group of friends to hang out with. But it never occurred to her that this might be any kind of problem until the new girl came to school.

Her name was Suzy MacGrizzie. It seemed like a funny sort of name. For one thing, it had a lot of Zs in it. The new girl herself seemed a little funny too. Her clothes weren't exactly cool, and she wore her hair up in pigtails, which was definitely not the standard Bear Country School style. Besides, she had thick glasses and braces—not the cool kind with lots of different colors like Millie wore—just plain old braces.

On her first day, of course, the new girl didn't know
anyone at all. At recess, Sister noticed her standing off
by herself in a corner of the playground. She looked sort
of sad and lonely. Sister was thinking about going over
and introducing herself when Lizzy and Anna came up.

"Hiya, Sister!" said Lizzy. "We're getting together a game of hopscotch. Millie and Linda are over there. Come on!"

Sister began to follow them. But she paused and glanced back to where the new girl was standing all by herself. The new girl looked lonelier than ever.

"Wait a minute," said Sister. "What about that new girl—that what's-her-name—the one over there? Maybe we should invite her to join in. She looks pretty lost and lonely."

The other girls were surprised.

"Suzy Whoozy-face?" said Lizzy, doubtfully.

"She has weird clothes," said Anna.

"And those corny pigtails," said Lizzy.

"Not to mention those clunky glasses and braces," added Anna.

"Well," said Sister, discouraged, "I just thought …"

"Oh, don't worry about old Suzy MacWhoozy!" said Lizzy, taking Sister's arm. "She'll be fine. She'll find some other cubs to play with—cubs more her type. Come on!"

Sister allowed herself to be led away to the hopscotch game. She felt a little worried about Suzy MacWhoozy, though she couldn't exactly say why. But she soon forgot all about it while playing hopscotch with her friends.

Later, when school let out, Sister got in line for her school bus. She noticed that the new girl was standing right in front of her. She was going to say hi, but then Lizzy came up behind her, and they started to talk. They went on talking as they got on the bus.

Suzy MacGrizzie sat right behind them. Sister and Lizzy went right on talking together. Sister played with her new locket as she talked, twirling it around and around in the air.

When the bus came to her stop, Sister gathered up her things to get off. But she felt a soft tug at her arm. It was Suzy MacGrizzie. She was holding something out to Sister.

"Here," she said shyly. "You dropped this." It was Sister's new locket!

"Gee," said Sister. "Thanks!" It was all she could think of to say.

Sister climbed off the bus and watched as it pulled away. She could see Suzy looking back at her from the window. Sister hung her locket back around her neck. What if Suzy hadn't noticed her drop it? It might have been gone for good.

Mama was waiting for Sister as she climbed the front steps. "How was school today, dear?" asked Mama.

"Oh, okay, I guess," sighed Sister, dumping her schoolbag on the armchair in the living room. She glanced up at the framed sampler of the golden rule over the mantel.

Somehow, the golden locket hanging around her neck felt heavier than before.

That evening at dinner, Sister was unusually thoughtful. She picked at her lima beans and stared off into space.

"A penny for your thoughts," said Papa as he fed Honey Bear.

"Huh?" said Sister, looking up. "Oh, I was just thinking about that golden rule inside my locket," she explained. "I don't really get it. What's it supposed to mean?"

"Well," began Mama. "Let me give you an example. Do you remember that trouble you had when Queenie first moved to town?"

Sister perked up and paid attention. She remembered it all too well.

"Do you remember how Queenie started an in-crowd but kept you out and made fun of your clothes and hair bow?" Mama asked. "Do you remember how badly you felt?"

Boy, did she ever! Sister started to feel hurt just thinking about it. Her lower lip began to quiver, and a tear came to her eye.

"All the golden rule is saying," Papa continued, "is that you shouldn't turn around and do that same sort of thing to someone else."

He paused to scrape some mashed potatoes off Honey's chin. "You should always treat other people the way you would like to be treated yourself."

"But I would never do anything like that!" said Sister. "Besides, I don't have an in-crowd."

"Oh no?" said Brother, who had been taking all this in. "What about Lizzy and Anna and Millie and Linda? You play with them all the time. But I never see you asking anyone else to join in!"

"That's different!" protested Sister, angrily. "I'm just playing with my friends! We're not trying to keep anybody out!"

"Of course not, dear!" soothed Mama. "I'm sure you and your friends would never dream of keeping other cubs out of your group."

Sister Bear grew very quiet. Now that she thought it over, she wasn't quite so sure—not so sure at all!

The next day at recess, as soon as Sister came outside, she looked around the playground for Suzy MacGrizzie. She soon spotted her, sitting off by herself under the big oak tree at the edge of the schoolyard and reading a book.

Sister marched right up to her. "Hello, Suzy!" she said brightly.

Suzy looked up in surprise. "Hello," she said shyly.

"I'm Sister Bear, and my friends and I are going to play some hopscotch," Sister told her. "Would you like to join us?"

Suzy's face lit up. "Oh, I'd love to!" she said with a big bracey grin. "I love hopscotch!"

"Terrific!" said Sister. "Do you want to see my locket?

"Sure!" said Suzy.

"Okay," said Sister. "Come on! I'll show it to you ... over there."

Sister took off, and Suzy chased her, laughing, across the playground to the hopscotch square where Lizzy, Millie, Anna, and Linda were waiting.

Sister's golden locket gleamed in the sun as she ran.

The Berenstain Bears®
Kindness Counts

written by Jan and Mike Berenstain

ZONDERVAN.com/
AUTHORTRACKER
follow your favorite authors

ZONDERkidz

Living Lights™

"The King will reply, 'I tell you the truth, whatever you did for one of the least of these brothers of mine, you did for me."
—Matthew 25:40

Brother Bear was a bear of many interests. He enjoyed sports such as baseball, soccer, football, and basketball. He liked to draw and paint, and he was interested in science. He had hobbies like collecting stamps and baseball cards, and he enjoyed fishing and playing video games. But the thing he enjoyed most of all was building model airplanes.

He started building models with Papa when he was very young. At first, they made simple plastic models. But, soon, they were creating flying models out of lightweight wood and paper. Before long, Brother could build models all by himself.

He kept building bigger and better models that could fly longer, farther, and higher. On trips to the park with Sister Bear, he always took along his latest model for flight trials. It was a thrill to wind its propeller for the first time, let it go, and watch it fly across the park.

One Saturday afternoon, Brother tried out his latest creation, a big model plane painted bright red called *The Meteor*. He set it down on the grass and wound the propeller. Sister joined some of her friends nearby. One of them was minding her younger brother, Billy. He was playing with a small model plane like the ones Brother had when he was little.

When Billy saw Brother's Big new plane, he came over to take a look.

"Wow!" he said. "That's beautiful!"

"Thanks! She's called *The Meteor*. I built her myself," Brother said proudly.

"Wow!" said Billy. "I wish I could build a plane like that."

Brother finished winding the propeller and picked up *The Meteor*. "Can I help you fly it?" asked Billy. Brother was proud of his models and careful with them too. They took a long time to build and were easy to break. If you didn't launch them just right, they could take a nosedive and crash.

"Well," said Brother doubtfully, "I don't know...," But he remembered how Papa always let him help out when they were building and flying model planes. That's how he learned—by helping Papa.

"Well," said Brother, "okay. You can help me hold it."

"Oh, boy! Thanks!" said Billy.

Brother knelt down and let Billy hold the model with him.

"Now, remember," said Brother, "don't throw it—let it fly out of your hands. Here we go— one, two, three ... *fly!*"

They both let go, and the big red *Meteor* lifted up and away, its propeller whirring.

"YIPEEE!" yelled Billy. "Look at it fly!"

But Brother was worried. *The Meteor* was climbing up too steeply. As they watched, *The Meteor* rose high above the park. It seemed to pause in midair. Its nose suddenly dipped down, and it went into a dive. *The Meteor* hit the ground with a nasty *crunch*!

Brother and Billy ran to the wrecked model. Brother sadly picked it up and looked at the damage. Billy's big sister and the others noticed the excitement and came over.

"Oh, no!" said Billy. "Is it my fault? Did I do something wrong? Did I throw it instead of letting it fly like you said?"

Brother shook his head. "Of course not!" he said. "You did fine. This is my fault. I didn't get the balance right. It's tail heavy. That's why it went up too steep, paused, and dove down. That's called 'stalling.'"

"Are you going to fix it?" asked Billy.

"Sure!" laughed Brother. "'Build 'em, fly 'em, crash 'em, fix 'em!' That's my motto."

"Could I help you?" wondered Billy.

"Now, Billy," said his big sister, "you're too young to help."

But Brother remembered how Papa always used to let him help. That was how he learned about model airplanes.

"That's okay," Brother told Billy's big sister. "I don't mind. I could use a little help."

So Billy came along to the Bears' tree house. Mama and Papa were pleased that Brother was being so kind to young Billy.

"It's just as the Good Book says," Mama said, "'Blessed are the merciful, for they will be shown mercy.'"

"Yes," agreed Papa, "and it also says in the Bible that a kind person benefits himself."

"What does that mean?" wondered Brother.

"It means that no act of kindness is wasted," said Papa. "Any kindness you do will always come back to you."

Blessed are the merciful, for they will be shown mercy.
Matthew 5:7

Every afternoon that week, Billy helped Brother work on the plane. He didn't know very much, but he learned a lot and he had lots of fun. Brother had fun too. He enjoyed teaching, and he liked having a helper who looked up to him.

The next Saturday, *The Meteor* was ready for another flight. Brother and Billy took it down to the park. Everyone came along to watch. They wound *The Meteor's* propeller, held it up, and let it fly. It lifted away and rose in a long, even curve.

"This looks like a good flight!" said Brother.

The Meteor flew on and on across the field. Slowly, it came down, landing clear on the other side of the park in a three-point landing. Brother and Billy ran over. It was in perfect shape.

"Hurray!" yelled Billy, jumping up and down.

Brother began to wind up the propeller for another try, but he noticed a group of older cubs coming into the park. They carried a lot of interesting equipment and wore jackets that said "Bear Country Rocket Club." Brother went over to watch. They were setting up a model rocket. They were going to fire it off and let it come down by parachute. Brother was excited.

"Excuse me," he said to the cub in charge, "do you think I could help you launch the rocket?"

The cub shook his head. "Sorry!" he said. "You're too young. It's too dangerous."

Brother walked away sadly. But he noticed that Billy was staying behind. He was talking to the older cub in charge. The older cub called Brother back.

"My cousin, Billy, tells me you let him help with your model plane," said the older cub. Brother just nodded. The older cub smiled. "That was cool. You seem to know a lot about flying and models. I guess you can help out."

So the rocket club
let Brother hold things for
them, carry things for
them, and squirt a little glue here
and there. He learned a lot
and he was happy. When
it was time to fire off the
rocket, they even let Brother
push the button.

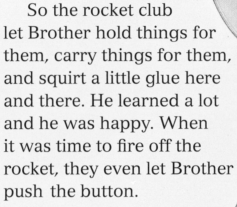

"10, 9, 8, 7, 6, 5, 4, 3, 2, 1 ... *fire!*"
said the cub in charge, and Brother
pushed the button.

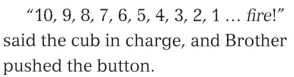

There was a loud *WHOOOSH*!

The rocket shot up, leaving a trail of smoke.

High above the park a yellow
parachute popped open, and the
rocket drifted back to earth.

They ran over to it. It was all twisted and scorched.

"Are you going to fix it?" asked Brother.

"Sure," laughed the older cub. "'Build 'em, fly 'em, crash 'em, fix 'em!' That's our motto."

"Could I help you?" asked Brother.

The older cub thought it over. "Sure," he said, slapping Brother on the back. "Why not?"

So, because Brother Bear had shown a little kindness to someone younger than himself, he became the youngest member, ever, of the Bear Country Rocket Club.

And was he ever proud!

The Berenstain Bears®

Go to Sunday School

written by Jan and Mike Berenstain

ZONDERVAN.com/
AUTHORTRACKER
follow your favorite authors

ZONDERkidz

Living
Lights™

"Blessed are those who hunger and
thirst for righteousness, for they
will be filled."
—Matthew 5:6

Sunday morning was a busy time in the big tree house down a sunny dirt road deep in Bear Country. The Bear family had things to do and places to go. Brother had soccer practice at ten thirty, and Sister had a ballet lesson at eleven. Usually Mama dropped them off before taking Honey Bear along to do some grocery shopping. Papa stayed home to get his fix-up chores done early so he could watch football in the afternoon.

But it hadn't always been that way for the Bear family. A few years back, before they'd gotten involved with so many activities, the Bear family had gone every Sunday morning to services at the Chapel in the Woods. Of course, that meant Brother and Sister went to Sunday school.

Mama Bear missed those days. It seemed to her that the family was a lot closer back then. Going to the Chapel in the Woods was like a kind of glue that held the whole family together.

Mama decided it was time for a little family conference. They all gathered in the living room one Saturday night, and she told them what was on her mind.

"Glue?" said Sister, puzzled. "You mean like when you glued that lamp back together after we broke it?"

"That's a very good example," said Papa. "That lamp gave us light. We glued it back together so we wouldn't be left in the dark. Worshiping God gives us light and warmth too. And our family needs a little glue from time to time to keep it together."

Sister and Brother thought that one over. It made sense … sort of.

"Besides," said Mama, "I believe that going to church together is more important than all our other Sunday morning activities combined."

"More important than soccer?" gasped Brother, shocked.

"Or ballet?" chimed in Sister.

"Yes," Mama nodded firmly. "But don't get too excited. We'll go to the early service at eight thirty. That way, you'll have plenty of time to get to your soccer and ballet."

"Eight thirty in the morning?" cried Brother and Sister, even more upset. "That means we'll have to get up at seven o'clock—on the weekend!"

"Now, now," said Papa. He prided himself on always getting up early. "Early to bed and first to get up, makes a bear healthy, wealthy and ... uh ... how does that go?"

"Sleepy!" said Brother.

At breakfast the next morning, the Bear family did seem sleepy indeed. At least Brother and Sister did. They could hardly keep their eyes open. Papa wasn't exactly all there either. He was almost invisible behind his Sunday paper.

"Coffee, dear?" asked Mama, lifting the coffee pot.

"Uh!" grunted Papa, holding his cup out without looking up.

"Ahem!" said Mama.

"Huh—wha?" asked Papa, looking up. "Oh, sorry, my dear!" he said, folding the paper. "I guess I'm not really awake until I've had my morning coffee."

After breakfast, Mama put on her best
Sunday hat. They climbed down the front steps,
and Papa put Honey Bear in her stroller. The
whole family headed down the road to the
Chapel in the Woods.

Other families joined them as they walked along. There were their neighbors Farmer and Mrs. Ben. They saw Uncle Willie, Aunt Min, and Cousin Fred from down the street.

They even ran into Too-Tall Grizzly being hauled along by his parents, Two-Ton and Too-Too Grizzly.

The Chapel in the Woods was nestled in a pretty little glen down by the creek. On this fresh spring morning, the dogwoods were in bloom. Papa began to hum a tune. Then he started to sing, "Come to the church by the wildwood. Oh, come to the church in the vale."

Mama joined in, "No spot is so dear to my childhood ..."

They finished together, "As the little brown church in the vale."

"What weird song is that?" asked Sister.

"Oh, it's just something we used to sing in church, together, when we were children," sighed Mama. "That was a long time ago."

"Did you know each other way back then?" asked Brother.

"Know each other!" laughed Papa. "Why, I was sweet on your mother when we were only eight years old. She was the cutest cub in the whole Sunday school. Once, I brought a frog into class. I was going to let it loose during the story of the plagues of Egypt. But I decided it would be funnier to slip it down Mama's back—it was too!"

Brother's and Sister's eyes widened, imagining the scene. "Wow!" they breathed softly.

"Now, dear," said Mama. "Let's not give the children any bright ideas."

They dropped Honey Bear off at the church nursery and filed quietly into the chapel. There was soft music playing on the organ as they found a pew. Then Preacher Brown climbed into the pulpit, and the service began.

"Welcome, friends!" said the preacher. "Let us join together in worship! Let us give thanks for this day the Lord has made!"

They all rose to sing a hymn. "Come to the church by the wildwood," sang the whole congregation. "Oh, come to the church in the vale."

After the hymn and a prayer, and a little more organ music and some bell ringing, it was time for Sunday school.

Brother and Sister joined the other cubs as they trooped out of the chapel under the watchful eye of Preacher Brown.

Old Missus Ursula Bruinsky was the Sunday school teacher. Brother and Sister wondered just how old she was. She looked old enough to have been Mama and Papa's Sunday school teacher.

"Good morning, children," she said with a big smile. "Today we're going to learn the story of Noah's Ark." She looked around at them brightly. "Do any of you young'uns know the story of Noah's Ark?"

Cousin Fred, who read the dictionary for fun, raised his hand.

"Excellent, Fred!" said Missus Ursula. "Why don't you tell us the story?"

So Cousin Fred told the story of Noah's Ark. "Long, long ago, God saw that the people of the earth had become wicked. But Noah was a just man, and he walked with God. So God told Noah to build a great boat—an ark. God was going to bring a terrible flood upon all the earth.

And God told Noah to bring two of every sort of creature, male and female, into the ark. So Noah built the ark, gathered the animals, and went into it with his family."

Brother Bear interrupted. "Do you think they brought frogs into the ark?" he asked.

Missus Ursula laughed. "Why, I'm sure that Noah brought frogs into the ark, Brother Bear," she said, her eyes twinkling. "But if you think that you are going to bring a frog into this classroom the way your father did, young man, you have got another thing coming!"

Brother's mouth dropped wide open. Missus Ursula really was old enough to have been Mama and Papa's Sunday school teacher!

Cousin Fred went on with the story. "Then it began to rain. It rained for forty days and forty nights. All the earth was covered with the flood. And all living things, except those on the ark, died. After many months, Noah sent forth a dove. The dove came back carrying an olive leaf. Noah knew that the flood had passed. He let all of the animals go. Then God set a rainbow in the sky and promised Noah that he would never cover all the earth with the waters of a flood again."

The cubs all sighed. They were thinking back to the last big thunderstorm they'd had when the river went up over its banks and washed out the bridge. There had been a beautiful rainbow after that storm too.

"All right, cubs," said Missus Ursula. "Let's see if you can all draw pictures of the story of Noah's Ark."

There were crayons and paper on the tables, so the cubs set busily to work. Sister drew a beautiful picture of the ark resting on the mountaintop.

Brother drew a dramatic scene of rain pouring down with bolts of lightning and the ark tossing on the waves.

Too-Tall drew a picture of all the animals sticking their heads out of the ark, yelling "PEW!"

"Now, Too-Tall," said Missus Ursula. "I really don't think that's very appropriate." But Sister noticed her smiling, just the same, when she thought none of the cubs were looking.

Then, Sunday school was over. "Goodbye, cubs!" called Missus Ursula. "See you all next Sunday!"

The cubs ran outside, shouting and jumping after sitting still for so long. The grown-ups were coming out of the chapel. Preacher Brown was shaking hands with everyone, and folks were laughing and talking together.

"There!" said Mama as they headed for home. "That wasn't too bad, was it?"

"No," said Sister. "In fact, it was kind of interesting."

"Yeah," agreed Brother, running on ahead. "And now ... soccer!"

"And ballet!" added Sister.

"And football!" said Papa.

Mama rolled her eyes.

Sister began to hum, then sing softly, "Come to the church by the wildwood. Oh, come to the church in the vale."

Papa began to sing along, in rhythm, "Oh, come, come, come, come ..."

And everyone joined in, "No spot is so dear to my childhood as the little brown church in the vale!"

"YAY!" shouted Honey Bear, wanting to join in too. And they all gave her a nice round of applause.

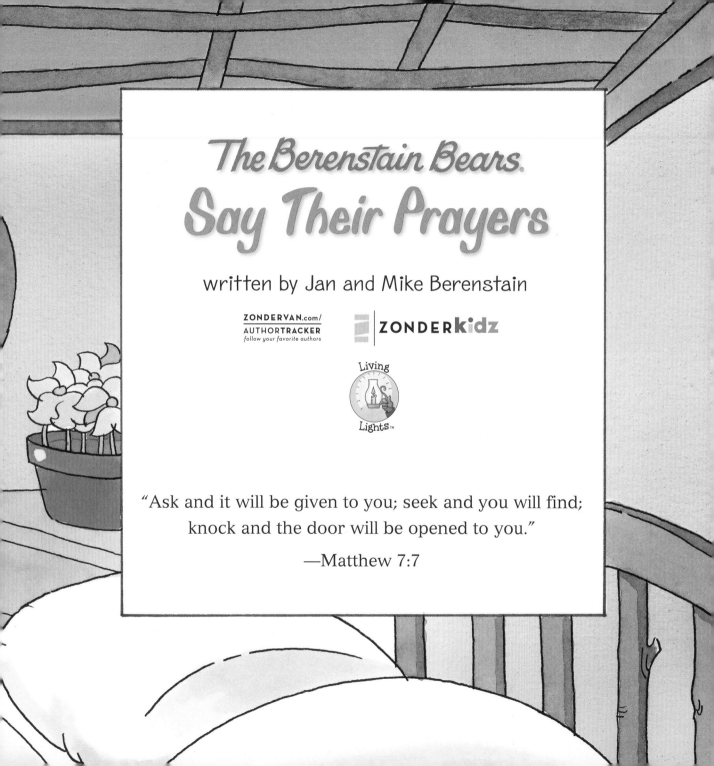

The Berenstain Bears
Say Their Prayers

written by Jan and Mike Berenstain

ZONDERVAN.com/
AUTHORTRACKER
follow your favorite authors

ZONDERkidz

Living
Lights™

"Ask and it will be given to you; seek and you will find; knock and the door will be opened to you."

—Matthew 7:7

It was bedtime in the Bear family's tree house—bedtime after a long, busy day. Little Honey Bear was already asleep in her crib. Brother and Sister were ready for bed too. They were bathed and they had their pajamas on. Mama and Papa were done reading them their bedtime stories. But there was one last thing to do before they went to sleep. It was time for Brother and Sister to kneel down beside their bunk bed and say their prayers.

Some evenings, they added a few more blessings like "bless our friends Lizzy and Barry" or "bless Teacher Jane and Teacher Bob." But when they started adding "bless Mayor Honeypot and Police Chief Bruno," Mama and Papa decided to draw the line. Mama and Papa were falling asleep before the cubs' prayers were over.

Tonight when Mama and Papa were giving the cubs their goodnight kisses, Brother asked a question. It was a question he had been thinking about for awhile.

"Mama," he said. "Why do we say prayers before we go to sleep? I was at Barry Bruin's house for a sleepover last week, and he doesn't say prayers at all."

"Some people just don't believe in saying prayers," said Mama. "But we pray at night so we can thank God for the blessings of the day."

"Do you and Papa always say your prayers before you go to sleep?" asked Sister, half asleep in the upper bunk.

"Not exactly …" said Mama. These days Mama and Papa were so tired at bedtime that they just flopped down and were snoring almost before their heads hit the pillow. "But I think it would be a good idea if we got in the habit again." Mama nudged Papa. "Don't you agree, Papa?"

"Huh?" he said, trying to stay awake. "Oh, right! Absolutely!"

"Good night now," said Mama. "Sweet dreams."

"Hmmm …" thought Brother, as he drifted off in the sleepy darkness. Mama's answer was okay. But he still had a few questions.

The next morning, Brother and Sister were up bright and early. It was Saturday and they had a Little League game. Their team was called the Sharks. They had a cool logo on their shirts—a big shark mouth full of sharp teeth.

"I feel hot today!" said Sister, tying her shoes. "I feel a whole lot of hits and stolen bases coming on!"

"Oh, yeah?" snorted Brother. "What about home runs? I guess I'll have to take care of that department!"

"Sure!" said Sister, punching him in the arm.
"Brother Bear, the Home-Run King!" She ran,
laughing, out of the room with Brother Bear chasing
her. Sister and Brother liked playing on the same team.
But sometimes they got just a little too competitive.

After breakfast, the whole family headed down to the ball field. Brother and Sister had practice before the game. It was Mama and Papa's turn to help with the snack bar. Papa was going to cook the hamburgers and hot dogs on the grill. Mama was going to sell candy and popcorn. Even Honey Bear would help out. It was her job to eat the leftover cotton candy. Papa soon had the grill behind the snack bar fired up. Mama opened up the candy stand, and Honey Bear started getting into the cotton candy.

The team ran out on the field for practice. Brother was playing shortstop, and Sister was at second base. Up on the mound, Cousin Fred would handle the pitching. Fred was a solid pitcher. But he had been struggling of late. His last two games were pretty shaky.

Today, they were up against the Pumas. The Pumas' uniforms weren't quite as cool as the Sharks'. But the Pumas were one of the best teams in the league. The Sharks would have their work cut out for them.

Since the Sharks were the home team, the Pumas were up first. Their lead-off batter was a big, powerful cub about twice Brother's size. He was twirling six bats around his head in the warm-up circle as if they were a bunch of twigs.

"Uh-oh!" said Brother. "Look who it is!"

Sister gulped. It was the Beast—the Pumas' best player. He could hit and field and pitch. They didn't know his real name. They just called him the Beast.

Brother glanced over at Fred on the mound. He had noticed too. He was taking off his hat to wipe his forehead. He looked pretty nervous out there.

"Play ball!" called the ump, and the game was on.

The Beast picked out a bat from his bunch and stepped into the batter's box. He took some warm-up swings and pounded his bat on the plate. He glared at Fred on the mound.

Brother noticed that Fred wasn't glaring back. In fact, he was standing quite still, his head bowed and his hands folded. It looked like his eyes were closed, and his lips seemed to be moving.

"Psst, Fred!" called Brother. "What's up?"

But Fred didn't answer. He straightened up, took a deep breath, and went into his windup. He fired a fast ball. There was a *swish* and a *thump*! The Beast had missed!

"Stee-rike one!" called the ump.

"Way to go, Freddy baby!" yelled Brother. "That's the way to pitch 'em in there! Just two more like that! You can do it!"

It was the sort of thing you always yell to encourage the pitcher. But did Brother really believe that Freddy baby could do it? It turned out that Freddy baby could.

There was another *swish*! and another *thump*! "Stee-rike two!" yelled the ump.

Another *swish* and a *thump*! "Stee-rike three!" called the ump. "Yer out!"

The batter had gone down swinging. The crowd in the stands cheered. The Beast kicked the dirt in disgust as he trudged back to the dugout

Fred didn't look nervous anymore. Now it was the batter's turn to look nervous. Fred threw six more fast balls to two more batters. There were six *swishes* and six *thumps*. Cousin Fred had struck out the side!

"That was some pitching, Fred," said Brother later on as they sat on the bench waiting to go up to bat.

"Thanks," said Fred.

But there was something else on Brother's mind. "I was wondering, Fred," began Brother. "What were you doing out there with your head down like that?"

"Oh," shrugged Fred, a little embarrassed. "I was just praying."

"Praying?" said Brother in surprise. "What were you praying for—strikeouts?" Before Fred could answer, it was his turn to bat. He trotted out of the dugout, leaving Brother still wondering.

By the end of the game, Papa had cooked thirty-three hamburgers and forty-seven hot dogs; Mama had sold three dozen lollipops and four boxes of chocolate bars; and Honey Bear was very, very sticky.

The Sharks were in a sticky spot too. They were behind by one run with two outs and a man on base. The "man" was Sister. She had gotten to first on a walk and then stolen second—she was a feisty little player. Now it was Brother's turn to bat. If he could get a hit, the Sharks might tie it. If he got a home run, they would win.

The Pumas' pitcher was none other than the Beast. As he walked to the plate, Brother felt a little sick. Talk about pressure!

Before he stepped into the batter's box, Brother decided to do something he had never done in a baseball game. He bowed his head, closed his eyes, and said a prayer. "Dear Lord," he prayed. "Please let me get a hit."

Feeling a little more confident, Brother stepped up to the plate. The Beast wound up and let it fly. Brother didn't even see it.

"Stee-rike one!" called the ump.

Brother gripped the bat tighter. He'd get the next one. Another scorcher screamed past.

"Stee-rike two!" called the ump.

Brother clenched his teeth. He was definitely not going to let this next pitch get past him. The Beast wound up, the ball flew, and Brother swung—hard!

Swish!—Thump! "Stee-rike three!" bawled the ump. "Yer out!"

The game was over. The Sharks had lost, and Brother had struck out!

"Way to go, Home-Run King!" shouted Sister in disgust. She was angry that all her efforts to get on base had gone to waste. Brother trudged back to the dugout, his head hung low. He had never felt so awful in his life!

Later, as he packed up his things, he found Fred standing next to him. "Don't let it get to you, Brother," said Fred. "That was a tough game. The Pumas are a good team."

"Yeah," agreed Brother. "I tried everything. I even tried praying like you did when you struck out the Beast. But it didn't work for me."

"Really?" said Fred. "What did you pray for?"

"I prayed for a hit, naturally," said Brother.

"Oh," said Fred, rubbing his chin. "I see."

"Why?" asked Brother. "What did you pray for?"

"I just prayed that I wouldn't get too scared," said Fred simply.

Brother blinked at him. "I guess your prayer was answered!"

"Prayers are always answered," said Fred. "Sometimes, we just don't get the answer we expect. Say," he added, sniffing the air. "Do you smell something burning?"

That's when they noticed the column of thick black smoke rising from behind the stands. "The snack bar!" they both yelled, and ran for it.

The smoke was coming from a batch of burning hot dogs on the grill. Papa was covered with soot and was trying to put the fire out with his hat. Mama came running up with a fire extinguisher. A few good squirts and the flames were under control. Honey Bear was laughing and clapping.

"Boy!" coughed Fred, waving the smoke away. "Maybe we should have prayed for rain!"

That evening at bedtime, Brother and Sister knelt down beside their bunk bed to say their prayers. Tonight, they felt like a nice long one:

"Bless Mama, bless Papa, bless Honey Bear, bless Grizzly Gramps, bless Grizzly Gran, bless Cousin Fred, Uncle Willie, and Aunt Min. Bless our friends Lizzie and Barry, and bless Teacher Bob, and ..."

When they were finished, Brother and Sister woke Mama and Papa up and climbed into bed. Mama and Papa kissed them goodnight, turned out the light, and went downstairs.

As Brother lay drowsily in his bed, he started thinking over the day's baseball game. If only he had been able to get that hit … or even a home run!

"That was a tough game today, wasn't it?" he said to Sister up on the top bunk.

"Yeah," answered Sister. "Tough on you, Mr. Strike-Out King."

"What's that supposed to mean?" said Brother, glaring up at the bottom of her bunk. "I played my best! A strike out like that could happen to anybody!"

But Sister didn't answer. She was fast asleep. Brother rolled over and ground his teeth. Sometimes Sister Bear made him so angry he could just … But then he thought of something. He thought of another prayer.

"Dear God," he prayed. "Please help me out with my little sister!" And to his surprise, he found his prayer had been answered. He didn't feel angry anymore.

"Thanks for the help up there!" he said.
And with a sigh, he fell asleep.

The Berenstain Bears.
God Loves You!

Activities and Questions from Brother and Sister Bear

Talk about it:

1. Why did the director and coach choose Brother and Sister as managers instead of for the parts they wanted?

2. What are some signs of God's love around you right now?

Get out and do it:

1. Draw or paint a beautiful rainbow, flower, or butterfly.

2. Make a photo album of people you love. Add cutouts, stickers, and drawings of hearts, rainbows, and stars to remind you that signs of God's love are everywhere.

3. Count how many times you can bounce a ball without stopping. Try bouncing it different ways and count (with a clap in between, with your other hand, between your legs, etc.).

The Berenstain Bears and the Golden Rule

Activities and Questions from Brother and Sister Bear

Talk about it:

1. When has someone treated you in a way you didn't like?

2. When have you treated someone in a way that wasn't very kind or fair?

Get out and do it:

1. Cut out a large construction paper heart. Write the golden rule on it and hang it on your bedroom wall.

2. Use chalk to draw a hopscotch frame on the driveway or sidewalk. Invite a friend to play with you.

3. Do something kind and unexpected for someone in your family.

The Berenstain Bears.
Kindness Counts

Activities and Questions from Brother and Sister Bear

Talk about it:

1. Do you have a special talent or hobby? How did you first become interested in this hobby? How did Brother become interested in model airplanes?

2. Why did Brother hesitate before actually sharing his model airplane with Billy? Why is it sometimes difficult to share something you really like and other times very easy?

3. Describe a time that you have shown kindness to someone and been shown a kindness in return. Do you think that you need to be rewarded every time you do something nice? Why or why not?

Get out and do it:

1. Create a poster for your family to hang in a prominent place in the house. Have the following scripture phrase on it: "In everything, do to others what you would want them to do to you." (Matthew 7:12)

2. Organize a family hobby day. Have each family member share what they enjoy doing the most with the rest of the family. Remember to be kind as you explain directions and show others your hobby.

The Berenstain Bears Go to Sunday School

Activities and Questions from Brother and Sister Bear

Talk about it:

1. How is the Bear family's church different from yours?
   How is it the same?

2. What are some things your family does on Sundays?

Get out and do it:

1. Draw or paint a scene from a favorite Bible story, or use
   magazine pictures to make a collage.

2. Draw and label four things you like about Sunday school.

The Berenstain Bears.
Say Their Prayers

Activities and Questions from Brother and Sister Bear

Talk about it:

1. What did Fred mean when he said, "Prayers are always answered. Sometimes we just don't get the answer we expect"?

2. How do you think Brother's prayer at the end of the book helped him with the problem he had with his sister?

Get out and do it:

1. Design a cool shirt for a sports team called the Bears.

2. Visit a park with a baseball field. Run around the bases. Name something you are good at or thankful for at each base.

3. Make up and memorize a prayer for bedtime. Say it every night before you go to bed.

"Your word is like a lamp that shows me the way.
It is like a light that guides me."

—Psalm 119:105 (NIrV)